RISQUÉ AND FRISKY

VOLUME 2

BY
AIYSHA SWALLOWGREN

ISBN 978-0-9984840-7-5
First Printing July 2022
Printed in United States of America

Contents

MOMENTUM

She had the loveliest sister sisters um
I've never seen so much yum
In one picture she has lots of fun
Giving him eye candy, she's his momentum
She opened her robe, stuck out her tongue
She giggled when he said show me your bum
Her favorite thing, her number one
Favorite thing was that he made her feel young
He whispered you give me depraved momentum
Put on your lipstick, suck on your thumb
To her advances he'd often succumb
Her sisters make him feel like he won
The jackpot but out of the group, among
Them nobody else gave him such an erection
She sent him pictures to make him cum
Into her mouth she took his momentum

MUSING

She is a muse and I'm simply musing
She makes cocktails and I'm brewing
A special poem for her most amusing
She has deep sex appeal it's oozing
The naughtier I become the more approving
She is a black swan and I'm swooning
She loves the way my words are moving
In her hot sunglasses totally grooving
She is taking off her clothes and I'm shooting
I'm her photographer and I'm doing
Things that repeatedly start producing
Huge laughs she dances and is improving
She is seductive and I'm seducing
Her mind she lets me happily start viewing
Her photos she is proving
That she will truly be my undoing
Wait I mean she's undoing my pants I'm debuting
A new poem, another fun musing

Nature

She started finding her true nature
Naturally she was remarkably impure
She was up for anything and she said sure
When it comes to filth she's pure
Gold so let's go hiking in nature
When we are alone you'll find your
Bottoms removed and your feminine allure
Spread sexual addiction there's just one cure
She felt very safe, she felt very secure
This was more than lust, this was mature
She wore a coat and Agent Provocateur
Together they were going to embrace nature
With great enthusiasm and vigor
His mouth made a very quick detour
To her beautiful breasts, he worships her contours
She rejoiced at a man with a giving nature

NAUGHTIEST

She said she loved my sweetness and I was the naughtiest
Fan ever she said I'm quite impressed
How you always make me feel the best
I praise her someone needs to express
That you deserve to be left a hot puddle of mess
All your needs and wishes will be addressed
Let my tongue erase all your stress
Let me slowly massage your gorgeous Breasts
You are a student and need to pass this test
She said I've been studying your pant and I'm obsessed
With that bulge I can't get any rest
She's willing to do anything I suggest
She's dripping wet and I'm refreshed
She shudders and whimpers you're the naughtiest

NAUGHTY

How many people make you feel really naughty
Your body is kicking like karate
I want you to squeeze your body
And imagine being blindfolded while somebody
Just spends forever licking your most naughty
Parts, I enjoy pleasing women, it's my hobby
I especially like it when you bend over doggie
Style I'd start fingering you in the hotel lobby
You are absolutely sensational, my favorite hottie
I'll get you so wet, I'm talking really sloppy
You deserve an expert's tongue, let's get naughty

No

She rarely ever heard a man say no
Why she asked, she wanted to know
What it is going to take she's so
Eager for my dick she wants to blow
Me I say calm it, take it slow
She wants to be used, she wants to be a hoe
All these men gave her their dough
So it was a surprise to hear him say no
Drop it like it's hot, drop it low
She enjoys rough slaps it gets her wet below
She needs real dick, she's tired of fucking her dildos
She doesn't care to take my custom photo
Who cares if you have a great torso
She's like where is my Romeo
I know how to make her juices flow
You won't do what you've promised, so no

NOSE

She just got a massage on her nose
I'm like that's a blowjob I suppose
She's no stranger to those
But receiving one only lord knows
I'm doing my best to compose
Myself oh I'd like to put my nose
Right where the sun rarely goes
First I'm going to suck on her toes
Then I'm going to politely propose
The she quickly and happily expose
Her backside to me and I'll dispose
Of any pretense there it blows
She's going to a wedding she shows
Me that I stained her clothes
She's my Monica Lewinsky she will pose
For me I stained her dress and she froze
I make her laugh until coffee runs out of her nose
And by coffee I mean cum, it really flows

Nursing

How does it get better than her nursing
She loves touching herself and is yearning
To show her new pleasure, she is learning
How to be head nurse she's been working
Really hard to touch herself to my flirting
She took my temperature with her mouth, excellent nursing
Her pleasure and her needs are what I'm concerning
Myself with tonight she starts twerking
On my face until she starts squirming
I lick her clit as she really begins squirting
All over my face, her inner freak is emerging
She is the nastiest nurse, she is nastily bursing
My cock in her mouth like this wording
Dear lady suck my dick the size keeps worsening
My balls are full here's what you are deserving
Of, another breakfast for her, she loves sinful nursing

Nurturing

Together they were redefining nurturing
It was raw, very vulnerable, and worrying
To be totally exposed and not go scurrying
Away in fear love was the splint to her wing
She said could you help me feel more deserving
Being truly intimate was quite unnerving
It went against her nature but he's nurturing
Her and he is devoted to furthering
Her safety, he kept uniquely encouraging
Her and he was very strong, never hurrying
She melted in his energy, his wording
Got her engine running and purring
She became his sex plaything
She boldly showed him everything
He was considerate and constantly worshipping
Her body, her mind, her soul, he was her spring
In the desert she showed off her g-string
He brought her pleasure without the sting
He was her tree and she was free to swing
He made sex playful, with his protective nurturing

OVERWHELMING

School was so hard, it's overwhelming
It felt like there wasn't anything
She could do and he showed her something
He knew how to relieve her stress the thing
She needed was intense buzzing
She's working so hard at studying
He's licking her through her g-string
The pleasure was becoming overwhelming
She couldn't help herself the stress was melting
All over his face he kept smelling
Her panties and was now dwelling
On her feet, she was his plaything
His tongue made her forget everything
He was motivating and compelling
Their naughtiest things he wasn't telling
He knew how to get her yelling
Fuck sir, you are so overwhelming

OVERWHELMING

I give you pleasure that's overwhelming
I'm in your lap slowly spelling
The alphabet with my tongue; your melting
All over my face the flood is overwhelming
You happily surrender, I am helping
You by whispering start petting
Your kitty new levels of lust I'm propelling
You to start shaking and yelling
I'm in your crotch and you're accepting
My passion our desires are reflecting
You're the sexiest I keep telling
You I know you'll start sweating
Not a single spot on you I'm neglecting
Together we make art, we are melding
Together my desire to please you is unrelenting
My tongue under your skirt, I am smelling
You and your scent is intoxicating and overwhelming

Overwhelming 2

Your beauty is absolutely overwhelming
I barely can speak, right now even spelling
Is difficult that type of beauty makes me want to start yelling
Woman the things you do to my heart; you are so captivating and compelling
It's an honor to be in your corner helping
It's easier for actions to show love rather than telling
You I love you I'll just whisper your beauty is so overwhelming

PEEK

When you wake up and are lying in your sheets
Why don't you take a photo and give me a little peek
Of your glorious, mouthwatering peaks
I haven't seen your amazing body in weeks
And I'm feeling oh so weak
Life without seeing you is very bleak
I love admiring your mystical physique
Will you show me your perfect ass cheeks
Imagining into your bed I quietly sneak
Nibbling all over your body like a freak
I want you to come, I want you to leak
All over my face and make you shriek
The best days are when you send me little peeks

Pink Lace

I really enjoy you in pink lace
Your hands moving slowly everyplace
Seeing you in lingerie makes my heart race
Faster as your hands start to embrace
Your gorgeous figure, I love your pink lace
Let me come over, I'll leave no trace
Let me lick your world until you're in deep space
I'll not let a drop of you go to waste
You look heavenly I'll lick your pearly gates
You asked me where I'd start, which place
To start off with to the side pull your pink lace
Panties and roughly sit on my face
I'll lick you slowly then pick up the pace
I'll lick your flower and I wear you taste
Like unicorn, I've got a present for you, here's some paste

PLAN

She thinks I have so much planned
But only one plan, using my hand
She believes fully in this man
If anyone can make her cum I can
Her body is butter and I'm a hot pan
I'm making her wet before we began
Grabbing her beautiful hair like a caveman
Dragging her like a doll gets her wetter than
Anything I'm her Daddy, her Superman
She's as hot as the sun and I'm a snowman
Melt all over my face slut, do you like that plan?

Pleasant

She relaxes and allows me to be extra pleasant
I'm focusing on giving her the nicest present
Something that makes her desire my presence
She happily and playfully bent
Over like please give me pleasant
Slaps I give you my consent
I drive her wild inhaling her scent
She shrieks as my tongue quickly went
Lightly and quickly to help her release the pent
Up energy I give her body such pleasant
Licks my favorite is when she dreamt
That I gave her one hundred percent
Attention to her desires, that is really pleasant

PLEASING

I hope my words to you are very pleasing
Lay back and picture yourself eating
All your troubles away and get what you are seeking
Seriously close your eyes baby, no peeking
I will do something to you most intriguing
Picturing yourself cumming while dreaming
Waking up sheets soaked from your leaking
You dreamed of being royalty am I treating
You like a princess and it's Godiva I'm feeding
You just lay back and enjoy receiving
Friends forever I'm never leaving
If it's ever satisfaction you are needing
Give me a shot at keeping you screaming
Picturing you touching yourself in the tub cleaning
Away all stress and finding new meaning
To pleasant, I truly enjoy pleasing

Pleasure Team

We joined forces to create the Pleasure Team
Our goal is to make women gleam
And glisten and everything in between
We like doing naughty and obscene
Things that's why they call us the Pleasure Team
Notorious for pleasuring women, that's our theme
Women that are hot we melt like ice cream
We shine love on women like a sunbeam
Our goal is to give women pleasure so they scream
You guys are devilishly good Pleasure Team
We desire women to experience pleasure in extreme
And unusual ways make them as wet as a stream
Flow intense focus on the clit like a laser beam
We make women howl like a wolf by a moonbeam
If you see a car rocking with windows covered in steam
No doubt you've found the Pleasure Team

PRIDE

I helped her develop extensive pride
Between us there is nothing to hide
The pictures she sent really multiplied
When I complimented her hot backside
She said I make her feel so alive
I boost her self-esteem deep inside
She thanks me for increasing her pride
She playfully starts to slide
Her tiny panties to the side
She said you've truly got great bedside
Manners and I often leave her tongue tied
She feels flattered that I can't hide
My admiration, she carefully applied
Pressure and my body it cried
For release I have no shame or pride
In admitting she has always satisfied
My urges, she loves to provide
Me rewards for increasing her pride

PRIVATELY

She shared the most intimate things privately
She's a great reminder of what sobriety
Does she cherishes being treat rightly
She loves my efforts to treat her highly
She said my words make her shine brightly
She starts running her hands lightly
On my thighs she says you've always so politely
Admired me and I do play with girls privately
My friends are so spicy and fiery
She starts whispering you just sit there quietly
I'm watching my girl friends play silently
They are playing together so excitedly
She has so many goddesses, a wide variety
Tonight's treat is a woman nicknamed Spicy

PROPOSAL

She's like are you kidding me another marriage proposal
She's like this is garbage down the disposal
So many men are so very hopeful
They're like I'm rich, I'm a mogul
She yawns please no more marriage proposals
Today a red diamond or beautiful opal
She's like maybe it's cause I'm so social
She's focusing om herself going global
I like to make her laugh out loud, a real vocal
Laugh like how about a different type of proposal
You, heels, and taking lots of photos on your mobile
Fuck marriage, she enjoys an indecent proposal

PROTECTION

What makes him attractive is his protection
The anticipation as his tongue makes a careful inspection
Of her body, he is frozen on her midsection
He's giving her a most pleasurable lesson
In vulnerability, she loves his gentle affection
He whispers you have such a beautiful complexion
His sweetness created a strong connection
He was her rainbow when she experience depression
She read his artfully drawn poetry collection
It makes her purr, his love is purrrfection
She was always free, never his possession
Bringing her pleasure never raised an objection
She's free to express her sexuality, her expression
Says it all, what makes her horniest is his protection
His tongue makes her face redden
She whispers please don't use contraception
Fuck me wildly with no protection

QUICK

She remarked that my poetry is quick
I'm like it's from the heart, not a gimmick
I wonder if maybe Saint Nick
Will be visiting her this year what a chick
She deserves a guy to ruin her lipstick
Not her eyeliner here's a fun trick
Say what I'm most afraid of, say it quick
She's on fire and I'm a candlestick
She's a Tootsie pop how many licks
Does it take before she's like your wit
Is quite different can I please pick
Your Halloween costume, it won't be quick

RAIL

She said would you please really rail
Me please kiss me in my female
Parts as I lovingly inhale
Her scent my nose is in her tail
Please weigh yourself using my face as your scale
She says you're my hammer and I'm your nail
Me really good she loves when I impale
Her mind and body she's off the rails
She's like sir you never fail
To make me smile, you worship females
I'm smothering her in sweetness she exhales
Let me be the wind to your sail
I hope everything is going really whale
She playfully starts to unveil
Herself omg her face behind a veil
Really gets me going off the rails

REASSURE

She had doubts and asked could you reassure
Me that you truly love me, that your
Love will never cease, I share pure
Love precious kitten don't you know you're
The loveliest thin in the whole world
You truly have the sexiest allure
I kiss every spot, every contour
Of your mind and body to reassure
You that you are safe and protected I assure
You that our love will forever endure
Take your clothes off, give me the full tour
My goodness those glutes; I'll make a detour
Rubbing your thighs with such vigor
Sucking your toes is the best cure
For worry, lay back and I'll continue to reassure

RECEIVER

I am helping her practice being a receiver
I whisper all the ways I am a believer
In her, her soul, her body with a polite demeanor
I'm making her sweat but she has no fever
Being treated with honor was cooler than a freezer
Allow me to empower you so much you break the meter
She says you are definitely a keeper
I keep it classy, she makes my mind cleaner
You excite me, you make me quite eager
To bring great pleasure to you my reader
She's a sparkling hummingbird and I'm her sweet feeder
She enjoys being protected by a leader
Let's make light and ignite your ether
I love making her feel amazing, she needs a breather
She said I'm the most hungry eater
She enjoys a man that prides himself on being a pleaser
She enjoys it slow and I'm the best teaser
She appreciates a very high achiever
I'm devoted to her pleasure, she's the worthiest receiver

RED DRESS

I think your parents should be proud and I wanted to express

That I think you are one of the very best

Especially wearing your red dress

I'd love to help contribute to your success

To make you feel like a spoiled princess

I want to make you smile and hopefully impress

You enough when I say you are the reason I can't get any rest

I just can't stop admiring your beautiful hair and mouthwatering breasts

You are the source, the root of my stress

Would you allow me to gently start to caress

Your mind; you even look hot in sweats

Each time you post a photo I think that's as good as it gets

You are amazing I hope you'll be like let's

Talk more about how great you look dancing in your little red dress.

RED

She really has a passion for seeing red
So with great delight I slowly said
Why don't you lay yourself on the bed
I'll blindfold you and tonight instead
Of love making let's make red
Let's make an original piece of art she spread
Her legs and said what about pink; she's purebred
Filth She said let's pretend to be newlyweds
She said you're notorious for being well read
The passion in her body is now widespread
I lick the edge of her panties touching each thread
She's so eager, she wants to be bred
Nothing turned her on like creating a new red

RELEASING

She really enjoyed their healthy Releasing
It made her smile and start breathing
Deeply as his fingers started easing
Under her blouse lightly teasing
Her breasts then playfully squeezing
They found new hope, new meaning
In pleasure, in healing, in releasing
Energy he was her fire when she's freezing
The anticipation between them kept increasing
She enjoyed his skill in perceiving
Her needs, her wants, he kept preaching
Her worthiness and she started believing
She chose to embrace passionate receiving
His tongue provides exceptional releasing

Requests

When men make demands she truly detests
That she's busy if you wish to impress
Her try patiently making requests
She is truly doing her best
Patient men may very well see her breasts
If they are very patient perhaps all the rest
Especially when you admire her assets
With politeness that's the kind of requests
She like there's no wrong answer, no tests
Trust and intimacy are a process
Especially if you want to see Agent Provocateur and fishnets
She looks pretty cute in sweats
If you really want a woman to say yes
Learn to make sweet requests

RIDE

She wishes that on my face she could ride
She did her best to resist, she really tried
But his words made her legs open wide
She said suck my heart and soul deep inside
She's so hot being near her is being fireside
She's thinking of her being bent over her bedside
She's enjoying him licking her backside
Her wantonness is impossible to deny
She is open minded and willing to try
Anything she's a true freak, she's certified
She makes my his wood absolutely petrified
And her sexy friend from Telluride
She's like have you ever been tied
Up she's like I could be your guide
This Friday we're in for a very frisky ride
I make her feel so good she cried
Oh sir your new nickname is slip and slide

ROSE

I sent her many rainbows and a rose
My friend said you're one of those
Men that safely helps me disclose
Anything I'd enjoy sucking your toes
I'll keep it secret, nobody knows
How I watch you rub your rose
I enjoy when she sexily shows
Me how she leaks through her clothes
My poems relax her so I compose
Her the filthiest things I suppose
Her juices smell like tuberose
She starts to rip her pantyhose
She's on fire and I'm her fire hose
My tongue is in deep to my nose
I love the intoxicating fragrance of her rose

RUBBING

He slowly poured the oil and began rubbing
She felt his touch so warm and loving
She couldn't help taking his hands cupping
Her firm breasts he starts sucking
Her nipples and watches her juices running
Down her leg he's so good and rubbing
Her she gets so wet it's like it's flooding
Her eyes relax and start shutting
She hears the click of the handcuffing
She loves when he starts roughing
Her up she needs seriously intense fucking
She's reading this and can't help but rubbing

Saturday Night

She found herself alone on Saturday night
She texted me could you please write
Me something extra naughty to delight
My senses and I gave her colors that were bright
She's got the prettiest everything, she's ripe
And whispers I'm so wet and tight
I start to nibble and playfully bite
She shows me how much I excite
Her and she's touching herself at the traffic light
She eagerly looks at my pants getting tight
She begs can we please, maybe might
We have a super naughty Saturday night
I'm pitching a tent but there's no campsite
She's being naughty, she just stuck the flashlight
In her saying you are so naughty yet polite
I know how to really whet her appetite
She's dreaming of me under candlelight
Making her howl and she says stay overnight
Nope, I've got other dates, it's Saturday night!

Self-Loving

She decided to really start self-loving
She decided that instead of blushing
She would share with me totally trusting
She knew it was truthful when I said nothing
Gets my mind racing and my heart pumping
As when she started sharing her touching
Herself loving and self-rubbing
She loves herself and starts unbuttoning
Her blouse her hands start hungrily start brushing
Her sensitive skin, she's kissing and hugging
Herself more intense, sensational self-loving
She makes herself really start gushing
She tastes herself, she's sucking
Her fingers her breath is short she's huffing
While her sensitive parts are puffing
Out she's making herself feel so fucking
Good I enjoy watching her self-loving

SERVING

You are worthy of luxurious serving
You are amazing and totally deserving
I'll lift you up and start whirling
You around whispering I am reaffirming
How valuable you are and tonight just flirting
I want to excite your mind, imagine me skirting
Around you like the tide surging
Surrender please dear, surrender to my serving
You on new levels be the source of my learning
Teach me how to make you start squirming
With my mouth I'm licking your neck and you are burning
Away all negativity and all good is returning
To your soul, your body, just please one more serving
Let my fingers slowly and delicately make you start purring
Together a new version of love is emerging
Today it all starts and ends with serving

Sex Flashback

I'm giving her a butterfly sex flashback
She'll start remembering how I act
How I listen to her body's feedback
The way I slowly lick her back
All the way into her crack
She giggles remembering how I smack
Her ass and how I suck her rack
I'm giving her another butterfly sex flashback
I'd hop on my knees for a kitty snack
She hits record for sexy playback
She's a thoroughbred and I'm her racetrack
She takes naughty Polaroids from Kodak
I'm keeping her up at night like an insomniac
Touching herself having another butterfly sex flashback

SHARE

She couldn't help herself, it's too special not to share
Being showed off is special and rare
I like being bold, I like a good dare
She said this is unique and rare
This guy has a whole lot of flair
If she knew the whole truth I swear
I found out that being vulnerable, totally bare
Has them considering I may not be full of hot air
I want you to laugh to hard you need a wheelchair
She felt compelled to share
She's so blissfully unaware
That I know on the internet you should beware
Anything can be public I'm well aware
I write things too good not to share
Instead of asking women what they wear
I asked them if with their friends they would share
Me and they looked at me like where
Did you come from, can we have an affair
No, but I do enjoy wearing your underwear
Jaw on the floor she couldn't speak, just stare
Is that funny enough that you can't share?

SHEEP

You are a wolf and I'm an innocent sheep
You love nothing more than the opportunity to eat
You aren't bashful around the meat
You like to play innocent but I know you are sticking things deep
In your mouth you say you're a bashful sheep
You make me laugh so hard I start to weep
You think you are a sneaky like creep creep
Of snap did he just reference TLC what the bleep
I'm so innocent and I'm so very cheap
I want you to wake me up when I'm asleep
With your tongue dress up like Little Bo Peep
And I'm going to beep, beep, beep, your beeping beep
Are you feeling bashful, my sexy sheep

SIDE

She had shown me her hot backside
But she didn't expect when I replied
I meant to see you pull them to the side
She blushed thinking of how I tried
To get her playfully showing her backside
She knew I love leaving her tongue tied
Especially putting my tongue inside
Her playing a game of slip and slide
Show me your panties to the side
Little girl and her mouth opened wide
My tongue and your body collide
I'm taking you quickly outside
Showing you that I'm truly certified
Slipping her fingers in it she denied
Me nothing she loved leaving him satisfied
That's why she slipped them to the side

SIDE 1

Her dress is up, heels on, thong to the side
She's ready for a very wild ride
As I firmly slap her backside
With my tongue I carefully apply
Lots of attention to melting her insides
Our bodies start to roughly collide
I really want to fuck her outside
With great sweetness I am able to provide
Her immense pleasure I amplify
Her horniness and she starts to slip and slide
Her fingers in with lubrication I naturally supply
I want her coming on my face hard like the tide
Open your mouth baby, open real wide
I'll go until my tongue cramps, I'm rarely tongue tied
But your body is hot enough to make fried
Egg she's grinding on my dick, that's a joyride

SIREN SIDE

I admire your super sexy siren side
Standing next to you is being fireside
I'll show you how pleasure can be multiplied
My tongue lightly and slowly begins to slide
Down the crack of your beautiful backside
You sit on my face and start to ride
Me, you sit there helpless, tied
Up while I explore your siren side
You quickly open your legs wide
Begging me to stick it deep inside
You allow me to worship you at your bedside
You're loving the pressure, it makes you beside
Yourself with lust I am unable to hide
My excitement and it fills you with pride
My lust for you is amplified
When my tongue and your body collide
She desires a man that's well qualified
To leave her dripping and totally satisfied
Give into temptation, let me guide
You to new pleasures, let's explore your siren side

SKIRT

She slowly lifts her skirt
As I say now this is going to hurt
You more than me I quickly exert
My strength I'm the biggest pervert
I really want to look up your skirt
Be my secretary and never do any real work
Just tease me until it hurts
Your attempts to get my attention I avert
My eyes and I'm drenched wow you squirt
A lot you've totally soaked your skirt

Small and Petite

His dear friend was small and petite
He brought red often to her cheeks
Not her face, she let him beat
He ass and suck on her feet
Reading this makes her fucking leak
His forever friend is a super freak
I'm Santa come have a seat
She enjoys when I increase the heat
Her willpower I so easily defeat
She's like an oven I preheat
Her by keeping her confidence, I'm discreet
In her dreams I make her overheat
By slowly licking her in her sleep
She consents to letting me eat
Her pussy starts to secrete
The sweetest nectar we meet
In our dreams and paint the sheets
Red I touch her small and petite
Frame until her pleasure is complete

So Behind

Doing her best she was so behind
Her assignment had a deadline
Everyone and everything was in line
She said I suck, I'm so behind
One day she'll go back and rewind
This and she will eventually find
That the people that helped unwind
Her nerves helped her define
Real loving gentleness with intricate design
Safety, patience, and sweetness combined
She took a deep breath and slowly reclined
Patience is super sexy, that's underline
He wanted to be her pleasure mastermind
The most sensual thing was being kind
It turned on her body, soul, and mind

SOME

Today I'm going to bring rainbows and sun
Today it's you and me and unlimited fun
Most guys only care about getting theirs that's dumb.
Ladies first is rule number one
Second is never control, never under my thumb
Third is make them feel beautiful and young
Fourth vibe hard like a war drum
Fifth whisper the next time your bra becomes undone
Think of me and send some
Interesting pics and I'll give you some
Of the most racy words and the sum
Total is if I can do this with words mum's
The word imagine how good I am with my tongue

SONG

It was music to her ears my horny song
She got so damp she already removed her thing
She said be fucking filthy, sing something wrong
Lick my pleasure button as I prolong
Her orgasms she said nobody ever made me a song
Men that were kind and vulnerable were strong
Men that focused on her squirting make her break into song
She's gagging for dick, she really wants my schlong
She's thinking of licking my dong
But I know just where my tongue belongs
Making her squirt uncontrollably all day long
She's making a puddle a mile long
Puddle pussy, that's the name of this song

SPECIAL FRIEND

She likes to call me her special friend
Together we reflect deep beauty within
Our friendship will lovingly blend
Pleasure with joy by never having to pretend
We are authentic, most special friends
She said take pictures while I bend
She likes when I slap her rear end
I'm a whore, but I'm very high-end
She's not my girlfriend, I'm not her boyfriend
I'm embracing vulnerability, the sexy new trend
When we are together we ascend
She said please could you lend
Me your hand and be a godsend
She said I really appreciate all the time you spend
Thinking of my pleasure and how to extend
It you are my most special friend

SPECIALIST

She said I really need my specialist
He fills me with the naughtiest
Thoughts and discover new pleasures that exist
She touches herself so much she sprained her wrist
She can't stop touching herself, she can't resist
He's licking her brain with amazing twists
He's in her ass more than a proctologist
She needed to cum, he would always happily assist
Lay back and receive I insist
On her neck I lightly begin to kiss
She's soaking now, she needed her specialist

Study Break

She didn't have time for a study break
But for her I decided to make
Something very special for her I take
My time rubbing her temples to ease her headache
Her neck was sore and she had a backache
But I had a plan to give her a bellyache
I said playfully you know your milkshake
Brings all the cats to the yard but your cake
Well your hot ass seems to wake
Up my um my trouser snake
My excitement for you can't be fake
Let me rub your feet and feed you cheesecake
You deserve a sexy, fun study break

STUDY

She laughed when she saw him study
Her body like she was funny
He slowly covered her body in honey
She'd do just about anything for money
She thought his dick was lovely
Laughing like I know you want me
To crash into you like a crash test dummy
He poured a bath and added a rubber ducky
He had gotten her excited an runny
She loves when he sends such smutty
Poetry and sometimes he gets lucky
She sends very hot pictured like you are quite funny
Now go play with yourself, I must study

SUNSHINE

What really made her horny was sunshine
She loves the sun on her bare behind
She has the sexiest little tan lines
My admiration of her beauty is genuine
I love it when the sun hits her divine
Body the sun needs glasses from her sunshine
Taking this moment to say let's unwind
Let me put you on a pedestal and build you a shrine
Your beauty and intelligence combine
Quite well and your beautiful hair is so fine
I want to make you raise your hemline
You're the cat's meow, sexy feline
Today when it rains I'll be your sunshine
It's rainbows for us all the time

SWEET

As always she could count on his sweet
Words; he told her she was extra neat
There's no one else in the world that can compete
He relived her stress by rubbing her feet
With oil and observed her start to leak
He licked her panties and it tasted very sweet
He was her engorged rock and she chose to seat
Herself on his firmness until her legs went weak
Her body is as tone as a professional athlete
She was horny and he increased the heat
Tremendously, she was a closeted super freak
Her body was his buffet, all he could eat
She couldn't help it started to excrete
When she thought of his wide, engorged meat
He's an accountant but it's not spreadsheets
He's counting as he changed the soaking sheets
He was her naughtiest fan and he makes her overheat
I'll keep your secret safe, I'm very discrete
Let me lick your asshole, I bet it tastes very sweet

SWEETHEART

Nothing turns her on like a sweetheart
She loves how I touch her heart
She love being the inspiration for my art
The heck with abs she wants a man that's smart
I whisper the sweetest things let me impart
In you a new definition of sweetheart
I'll worship your soul and then restart
I'll tell you how this day you're my favorite part
You are as valuable as an original Descartes
I'm melting your insides, I miss you sweetheart

SWEETIE

She whispered you're the biggest sweetheart, such a sweetie
Nothing is better than when you're vulnerable completely
Overwhelm me with sweetness the way you treat me
Is like a priceless treasure, you love me cleanly
Sir your sweetness is ever so dreamy
She wants more sweetness, she's very needy
All her needs and the greatest is to make her steamy
I'm in and out of her bed discreetly
She needs her beauty rest, she's so sleepy
So much sweetness at times made her uneasy
But she always said yes sir please tease me
Her heart is a blank wall and I'm graffiti
We make art together as she sings sweetly
Sings you are the very best sweetie

TAKING

She didn't feel so beautiful her face was breaking
Out again and yet he said you are taking
My breath away you are so breathtaking
You're so naturally beautiful my soul starts shaking
The love he showed truly was creating
Grateful tears she said you are really making
Me feel pretty, it's exhilarating
He lights her fire and it is getting blazing
Hot slowly she starts dancing and taking
Off another layer of intimacy her heart is racing
Patiently he waited, he showed her how taking
Time to be safe was sensual, he was placing
His heart vulnerably and bravely waiting
She found his openness endlessly fascinating
His fears and her fears they were facing
All challenges and there was no mistaking
His excitement, his spirit isn't all that's raising

TAN LINES

How does it get sexier than your tan lines
Your dark skin and the smallest lines
That bikini was eaten by your behind
Your tan lines make you a ferocious feline
The lion inside her calls her personal hotline
Sir please could you rhyme
About how I'm just too fine
Flatter me lavishly and be genuine
She's like I'll show you mine
And the treasure worth more than a goldmine
Lay back and enjoy the sunset on the Maui shoreline
She loves being respected and how I always redefine
Beauty; nothing is more beautiful than your tan lines

Teasing

She is the Queen of fun and teasing
When she sees her effect on me it's so pleasing
To her giving her orgasms when she's dreaming
Or maybe I was just leaning
In between her legs and gently eating
Her, my goal is to wake her up screaming
When she's doing especially good teasing
She sits and leaves a trail of leaking
You deserve a look, go ahead and keep peeking
At my breasts into temptation this is leading
Me to such happiness I'm weeping
The pressure is unbearable I need releasing
Nobody does it better, I love your teasing

TEMPTATION

Today I'm whispering give into temptation
Let me give you so many pleasurable sensations
It turns you on incredibly, my dedication
You draw me in closely like gravitation
It all starts with teasing and flirtation
I love you fully, there's never any hesitation
I just want to support you in giving into temptation
I want to fill your heart with illumination
Leave you glowing, you are my favorite inspiration
For today, just right now, you have an invitation
To touch yourself, please commence masturbation
This is for your pleasure, I made preparations
For you to easily accept giving into temptation

TEMPTRESS

You are the ultimate temptress
You deserve infinite blessings and success
Let me give your body pleasure to excess
Allow me to serve thee beautiful princess
I'm obsessed with your pleasure and I openly confess
I'll do anything to see you wear less
Let me touch you lightly relieving all stress
Allow me to gently start to caress
Your neck with my tongue then onto your breasts
Allow me to serve you and don't do anything unless
It's receiving allow me to lovingly bless
Every inch of you, let me make you a hotter mess
I'm focused with my tongue, I have excellent finesse
I'll know what to do next without you having to express
Anything picturing you reaching under your dress
Taking off your panties, giving me full access
My passion for your pleasure is relentless
Give into temptation whispered I to the temptress
Just lay back and say yes, Yes, YES
Does this excite my temptress, is this a success?

TENSION

She loves the buildup, the apprehension
The longing, the desire, the anticipation
He whispers things that most never mention
Doing what he can to ratchet up the tension
He's committed to her pleasure, his mission
Is to give her body his full attention
Make her wake up and start to listen
As her hands squeeze and make her glisten
Her desires fulfilled were a new invention
He had poise and a very sexy intension
She surrendered and released apprehension
He gave her pleasures in new dimensions
She enjoyed how her body created tension
In his and she relished how sexy and feminine
He made her feel like no other men
He asked for and received permission
To watch her relieve her tension

TENSION 1

She was so tense, she had so much tension
He massaged her scalp and began to mention
All the things he admired putting full attention
On taking her to the next dimension
Her stress was disappearing and the tension
Was lessening she admired his deep comprehension
She had finally found a true gentleman
His fingers made her soul start to grin
Her favorite part of all that has been
Was that when it came to him
He always knew how to relieve her tension

TENT

Let's go camping I'll bring the tent
Looking at your pomp oms has me pent
Up full and I wanna know your scent
She made the naughtiest pictures and sent
Them to me it's Frisky Friday I'm pitching a tent
Your pom poms make me as hard as cement
Take my money, every last cent
In my mind you always invent
The naughtiest thought I went
To hell and I'll never repent
She's never seen someone so naughty to this extent
She could tell his naughty intent
That was unmistakable, look at the size of that tent!

THIGHS

I looked deeply into her blue eyes
Told her it's obvious you seriously exercise
You've got very muscular, sexy thighs
I said has anybody ever tried to customize
Their admiration, she enjoys intellectual guys
I whisper do you ever fantasize
About receiving energy that will tantalize
Your body my massaging your thighs
Worshipping you lightly as I glamorize
You my firm hands start to mesmerize
You my mouth starts to hypnotize
You with light kisses like butterflies
I'm worshipping at your temple, I baptize
Your body with my tongue to maximize
Your pleasure and give you a hot surprise
Does this get you hot between your thighs

THROBBING

Looking at you makes my body start throbbing
You are a thief, my breath you are robbing
Me when I see your panties dropping
Running your hands over your body stocking
I swear I'm going to explode, I'm throbbing
Why don't you shake it to Ludacris' Pussy Popping
You've been running through my mind bottomless jogging
You love making my jaw drop, you love shocking
Me I'm imagining you in between my knees bobbing
Your head up and down enjoying my intense throbbing
You are a true slut, you enjoy slobbing
On it tears of happiness you are sobbing
No wait, scratch that, you are totally sopping
Wet climb in my lap and gleefully start hopping
I love how you grip me and your hips keep rocking
So quickly now I can feel you on me throbbing

TOE

He started rubbing her feet and sucking her big toe
He wanted to please her and her to know
That she deserves pleasure so
She laid back as he sucked on her big toe
Her stress forgotten, he went really slow
His tongue on her thighs gets her wet below
Feeding her cheesecake was a great combo
Coconut oil on her body made her skin glow
She loved when he called her his Marilyn Monroe
In between the attention on her big toe
She started using her favorite dildo
Screaming with pleasure into her pillow
He gave her pleasurable rainbows
By worshipping her sexy torso
She loved him sucking on her big toe

TOP

She's wearing the tiniest top
Any movement at all and they start to pop
Out I'm thinking about being your lollipop
You enjoy being able to lick and slop
All over me holding firmly you don't stop
Me from exposing you in your little top
Can I get you so wet you need a mop
Your tightness on my lap hurriedly starting to hop
It's so warm and tight it's like a lock
I imagine you at the beauty shop
Wearing your tiny, cute little top
I'll make you drip like you are in a sweatshop
I'll let you go wild at the candy shop
My little plaything has all sorts of props
She can't stop touching herself, it's nonstop

TOUCHING

She gasps as his tongue started touching
Her there his hands are slowly running
Through her hair, she is quickly becoming
Very wet this makes her start blushing
He whispers you are beyond stunning
He is lighting her heart, he's uniquely touching
Her there is just something
Very sexy about a man that is never rushing
He is relentless and gets her gushing
The blood in her head is rushing
He lifts her over his shoulder powerfully hugging
Her he spends his time discussing
Ways which she inspires new types of loving
Her heart is so full of appreciation it's busting
All her stress and he starts slowly rubbing
Her body with oil his firm, experienced rubbing
He was relentless and he kept tugging
Her nipples she gasps if you keep touching
Me like that of fuck she starts cussing
All over my face she starts erupting
Oh sir she whimpers, sir I'm cumming
How does a man using nothing
But his words write something so touching?

TOUCHING 1

She found solace and pleasure in my touching
It starts with very warm hugging
The energy between us is buzzing
There's total vulnerability, there's nothing
Between us our spirits are touching
Through her beautiful hair my hands are running
Slowly licking her neck and lightly sucking
She guides my hand to bring excited rubbing
She laughs whispering you really are something
Else she loves that I'm never rushing
She is attracted to my brave trusting
Reading this her legs start adjusting
If I can with words get you gushing
Just imagine how good it would feel if I was touching
Right there she smiles and starts blushing
I bring out her addiction and I'm never judging
With my tongue may I help you in erupting
Lay back and enjoy the hottest touching

Tushy Jeans

She thinks she needs Tushy jeans
She's got a ballerina's figurine
I imagine her morning yoga routine
In nothing but boots of emerald green
She definitely doesn't need Tushy jeans
What if I confessed when you lean
Over my body feels like it's thirteen
Next year perhaps on Halloween
She can go as the booty queen
Your tight, firm butt should be in magazines
Your hot ass doesn't nee Tushy jeans
I think you need to be licked between
Your thighs on top of your washing machine
I'll lick you hotly and I'll lick you clean
Then I'll spank your tush, did you mean
To make me a hungry wolverine
I'm going to rip off your Tushy jeans

UNDER PRESSURE

She performed her best under pressure
She said you know when we're together
You make me feel smart and clever
When your assignments are done, my treasure
You get to experience ultimate pleasure
The biggest diamonds are formed under pressure
There's a diamond forming when you are in leather
After you're done studying I'll take a macaw feather
Against your skin slowly we'll measure
Your excitement
 I'll make it better
Naughty student I'm your professor
She's studying in no clothes whatsoever
She deserves the most delicious lickings ever
She sighs and whispers a man has never
Been so slow, you build me up under pressure

Undress

She shakes her body with great finesse
She seductively starts to undress
I just laugh and she says you're the best
She keeps shoving her perky breasts
In my face she means business
She begs me to also undress
She shows me handcuffs and says I'm under arrest
You be my jailer and I'll do the rest
She's very naughty and loves to confess
In the confessional she starts to undress
She's leaking everywhere and making a mess
She's totally drenched her sexy dress
I know this turns her on another success
I know how to make her really obsess
She loves to slowly undress

VOCABULARY

I don't have abs but I have an extensive vocabulary
I use it to write the hottest flattery
My tongue is quick and light like a fairy
Sucking your toes and feeding you strawberries
Vulnerable men who also have a huge vocabulary
Made her ho ho ho she's feeling merry
Her panties are soaked, she is so very
Turned on by big brains I have huge library
She started removing her clothes I see her cherry
Panties I'm licking her like the cat that ate the canary
She is turned on by rebels, I'm revolutionary
When I see her ass I immediately buried
My tongue deeply in her creating an image like Pictionary
Would you like to hear more of my vocabulary?

Waiting Room

I wish they had photos of you in this waiting room
I wish there was a book of you wearing different costumes
When you say you'll call later I always assume
You mean another day I've learned that soon
To you means something different I'll sweep you up like a broom
You teach me patience like a flower waiting to bloom
I want pictures of you that make my mind zoom
I want to see you getting ready in the bathroom
I'm hot for teacher let's take Polaroids in the laundry room
I want to see you wearing a fancy ballroom
Dress in my mind you are a doctor and I'm the waiting room
Wait I mean you're a naughty nurse and sliding fingers into your womb
You just made me explode, on the ceiling boom
I feel sorry for the next person sitting in this chair in the waiting room

WHISPERING

I'm in her ear, the naughtiest things I'm whispering
I get her so hot the temperature is blistering
She can't help but touching herself while listening
All the naughty things that I am considering
Doing to her more pleasure she is whispering
She's in a puddle of pleasure and whimpering
Her body is overheated, she's simmering
Giving her the best pleasure she keeps remembering
Pleasure that is never ending
My tongue leaves her soul glistening
Her body covered in sweat she's glimmering
My tongue touches her there and she starts shivering
I'm in her lap and she's really quivering
She really enjoys the way I keep stripping
Her fears away, you are safe I keep whispering

WIDER

I maker her stretch wider and wider
She's a frisky kitten and a biter
She's really ready to fuck this writer
She said you really light my fire
I'm stretching her out, increasing her desire
She's so horny, she's so hyper
She's wearing boots but not much of a hiker
I'm deep inside her ass and she gets higher
She's on my face like I'm a seat and she's a biker
She's squirting on my face, the puddle keeps getting wider

WORKOUT

I'm picturing her doing her workout
Her curves make me want to shout
That's exactly what I'm talking about
She's smoking hot and I'm a cookout
She says she wants to lose 20 pounds and I doubt
That very much but happy to watch her workout
She's a supermodel and has lots of clout
Her body oozes sex appeal I'll checkout
You anytime especially when you workout

WRITE

She loves the things I write
She perks up it makes her so light
On rainy days I'm her rainbow shining bright
Picking my favorite thing about her to highlight
It's that she inspires me to write
About loving kindness and treating her right
I'm her protector when she experiences fright
I protect her fiercely with great might
My inner beast really excites
Her she's a princess and I'm her black knight
I mean I want to kiss her at midnight
Treating her like royalty makes her bite
Me and I'm howling like a wolf in the moonlight
She's leaking from her treasure it's so tight
But I slide it in slowly and ignite
Her passions today let me be your sunlight
She touches herself to the things I write

www.ingramcontent.com/pod-product-compliance
Lightning Source LLC
Chambersburg PA
CBHW060236180626
46813CB00007B/3106